STORY KEEPERS

Starlight Escape

Titles in
the Storykeepers series

Starlight Escape

Brian Brown and Andrew Melrose

ZondervanPublishingHouse
Grand Rapids, Michigan

A Division of HarperCollinsPublishers

For Abbi and Daniel

Starlight Escape
Copyright © 1997 by Brian Brown and Andrew Melrose

Requests for information should be addressed to:

Zondervan Publishing House
Grand Rapids, Michigan 49530

First published in the UK by Cassell plc, London.

ISBN 0-310-20337-6

Printed and bound in Great Britain by Cox & Wyman Ltd,
Reading, Berkshire.

Contents

Chapter 1

A Star-Spangled Sky

"Oh, Ben," whispered Helena, "look at the moon! It is such a beautiful night. So peaceful. For once, no danger."

Ben smiled at Helena and squeezed her hand as they bumped along in the wagon. They were a short distance outside of Rome on the road leading toward Ostia, a city near the sea, near the mouth of the Tiber River. For a change, Ben was not driving. He had left his bakery wagon at home.

The clip-clop of the horse's hooves on the paved road was a comforting sound. The hard wagon bottom was not. Helena, adjusting her position a little to find a more comfortable spot, said, "I wish sometimes we could travel in a little more style. This wagon is so uncomfortable."

"I know what you mean," chuckled Ben. "You need more padding, like me. Here, just lean against me."

They rode on in silence, enjoying the slow ride. They had plenty of time. If any Roman soldiers stopped them, they would seem like any other family on a trip. Or so they hoped.

Little Marcus, who was four, was curled up in Ben's lap, sound asleep. His thirteen-year-old brother, Justin, was sitting between Anna, who was nine years old, and Cyrus, who was eight. Before he came to live with Ben and Helena, Cyrus had been a circus performer and juggler.

Zakkai, Ben's sixteen-year-old apprentice, was riding on the wagon seat with old Milo, the driver, keeping an eye out for trouble.

Zak heard them first. Then he saw them—four Roman soldiers on horseback on the road ahead, galloping toward them.

"Oh, Ben," said Helena, who also had heard the approaching horses. She peered out the front of the wagon, straining to see in the darkness.

"Just sit still. Don't look frightened," Ben said.

The soldiers stopped in a line across the road, blocking their way. "Halt!" one shouted.

"Whooa," Milo said softly as he pulled gently on the reins. The horse stopped, head down, then looked back at Milo, as if expecting some secret signal.

"Where are you going?" the soldier asked.

"To Ostia," Milo said.

In the wagon, Ben, Helena, and the children almost didn't dare breathe. The Emperor Nero had ordered Roman soldiers to search for Christians and arrest them.

Many had already been captured. Thousands had been sold into slavery or thrown to the lions.

"What is your business?" the soldier asked gruffly.

"We are going to see my brother, who is ill," said Milo. "We are both very old. He does not have much time."

The soldier nudged his horse forward and looked first at Milo and Zak, then into the wagon at Ben and Helena and the children. He rode all the way around the covered wagon, while the other soldiers sat very straight, looking ahead, not moving a step.

Finally the soldier joined the others. He studied Milo carefully, then said, "Be on your way."

"Thank you, sir. Thank you," said Milo, and with a flick of the reins urged Regis to resume his slow, plodding gait. No one said a word until the soldiers had ridden out of sight.

Zak left his perch and moved back into the wagon, crouching next to Ben and Helena. "Ben, this road is too open. We're sitting ducks!" he said, his voice rising. "There's no place to hide! The moon is too bright! We were lucky that time, but they might come back. Nero's soldiers can spot us a mile away. We should never have taken this road."

"Well, we fooled those soldiers," Ben said.

"We might not be so lucky the next time," Zak said in a disgusted voice. "And as for Milo, he must be eighty if he's a day. Where did you find him?"

"Don't be ungrateful, Zak," said Ben softly. "It was kind of Milo to give us a lift in his wagon."

"But he's strange, Ben," Zak insisted. Darting a glance at the old driver, he said, his voice low, "And I'm not sure I trust him."

Chapter 2

Risky Road

"What do you mean by that? Calm down, Zak," Ben said. "Our friends told me that if anyone can get us to Ostia safely, it's Milo."

"I don't see how," Zak said, becoming even more agitated. "He talks to that old horse as if the horse can talk back to him. Calls the horse Regis."

"What's wrong with that?" asked Justin, who was particularly fond of horses.

"Yeah!" chimed in Anna and Cyrus.

"I like Milo," said Cyrus.

"Me too," said Anna, looking defiantly at Zak.

Ben did not like seeing the children ganging up on Zak and was about to interrupt when he heard Milo say, "You've got it all wrong, Regis."

"See, Ben?" whispered Zak. "He's talking to the horse again."

"We go left at the next junction, not right," continued Milo.

Ben and Helena and the children just looked at each other, then at Zak.

"Oh, well," Ben whispered, "just as long as we get there safely."

Zak went back to his perch next to Milo and scanned the countryside, looking for more Roman soldiers.

Ben and Helena were part of a secret underground network of Christians who risked their lives to help one another and to spread the stories of Jesus. They would meet in homes or even in caves, telling of Jesus' work. Danger was always with them.

"These children have had to grow up fast," said Helena, stroking the hair of little Marcus as he slept in Ben's lap.

"Yes," said Ben. "They've been through more danger in their young lives than most Romans see in a lifetime."

"Yes," Helena said as she snuggled back against Ben's shoulder. "We sometimes forget just how young they are. Especially Marcus. Poor little mite. He looks worn out."

Ben smiled at Helena and leaned back against the side of the wagon. They were not the children's parents. The children had been separated from their own parents when the Emperor Nero had ordered the city of Rome to be burned, then blamed the Christians for the fires.

In the days and weeks that followed the fires, Ben had found the children, living on the streets, dirty and hungry. They didn't know if their parents were alive or dead. Ben had taken them in to his warm bakery and given them a home.

As the wagon moved on toward Ostia, Anna, Cyrus, and Justin sat together at the back of the wagon, staring up at the blue-black night sky. Thousands of stars flickered in the darkness.

"Look," said Anna wistfully, "it's so beautiful. The stars are so bright tonight. I've never seen so many of them! Why don't they look like this at the bakery?"

"Because there are too many lights," said Helena. "And smoke from fires. The air in Rome isn't clear like it is out here in the country."

Little Marcus stirred and yawned and opened his eyes. It was getting late, and he was very tired. "Ben, why are we going all the way to Ostia for a story meeting?" he asked, then snuggled back against Ben's soft paunch to await the answer.

"Because it's getting too dangerous in Rome, Marcus. As more and more people become Christians, Nero sends even more soldiers to try to arrest us."

"Oh," said Marcus sleepily. "I miss the bakery. I like it there, especially by the oven. It's warm. And I can always have a piece of bread or a pastry. I like pastries better. I'm hungry."

"Well, Ben," said Helena, "it sounds as though Marcus is going to get as big a tummy as you."

Ben laughed as Marcus cuddled in. "We'll eat soon, Marcus. It's only a short ride. And we'll go back to the bakery as soon as it's safe."

"Promise?"

"I promise, and I won't let you out of my sight until we do."

Marcus sighed contentedly and went back to sleep.

"Eh? What's that you say, Regis?" Milo said to his horse. "Roman guards, you say?" Milo sniffed the air. "Well, I sure don't smell any guards."

Zak rolled his eyes and turned to look back at the others. "Well, that's a relief. Milo doesn't smell any—"

"Guards!" shouted Cyrus, pointing out the back of the wagon. "It's another patrol! Three horsemen!"

Chapter 3

A Wild Chase

"Well, well, Regis," said
Milo, giving the reins a flick.
"Looks like you were right
after all. Hold on, everybody, we're going for
a high-speed ride!"

Milo cracked the reins harder this time, and Regis
took off like a shot.

"Hey!" said Zak, clutching at the bench. "I nearly fell
off!"

"Then hold on. You were warned," said Milo.

"They're gaining on us!" Cyrus shouted.

"They've seen us and are giving chase!" yelled Ben
over the clatter of the horse's hooves on the
cobblestoned road.

"Hupp!" called Milo. "Hee! Hee! I love a good race."

"Let's hope you like to win," said Zak. "I don't fancy
being served to Nero's pet lions for dessert."

"Milo!" shouted Cyrus. "They're still gaining on us!"

"Don't worry. Your little juggling hands are safe with
me. I'll lose them."

Zak said, "If you have any tricks up your sleeve, Milo, you'd better use them right now."

"What? Right? What's that you say? You want me to go right? Why, only a half-witted goat would go right! We want to go left! Hold on, youngster."

Zak grabbed to get a grip on something but was too late. Milo turned sharply left, steering the horse through a break in the trees. As the wagon tilted, then hit a bump, Zak tumbled backwards into the wagon with the others.

"Wha … wha … hey, we've left the road!" Zak said. "What is that old goat playing at?"

"Shh!" said Ben.

Just then the three Roman soldiers rode past on the main road, unaware that the wagon had turned off and now was hidden behind the trees.

The horse and wagon sped down a steep, bumpy, and thickly wooded slope.

"Now we're in an olive grove," complained Zak as a branch on a huge olive tree scraped against the wagon. "I don't believe it. Are you trying to get us all killed, old man?" he yelled at Milo.

"Sit down!" shouted Milo, getting annoyed by Zak's persistent complaining.

Anna grabbed at Ben's arm. "Look, Ben, look! We're heading for that—"

"Milo! Look out!" yelled Ben.

Chapter 4

Starlight Campfire, Burning Bright

The horse was skidding on the steep slope, trying to stop, but the heavy wagon kept rolling, faster and faster.

"We'll tip over!" Helena cried.

Milo, his feet braced against the front board, pulled back on the reins as hard as he could. "Whoa, Regis! Whoa!"

The wagon slid sideways and there was a cracking sound as it skidded to a stop at the edge of a steep riverbank. A few inches more and the horse and wagon, with everyone in it, would have rolled over into the dry riverbed.

"Phew!" said Helena. "That was a close one."

"Yahoo!" cried Milo. "What a ride!"

"Is everyone okay?" asked Ben.

"I think so," replied Helena.

"But the wagon's not," said Zak, jumping down. "Look at this front wheel. It's broken. So much for our story meeting. We'll never get to Ostia now."

Milo climbed down from the wagon, walked to the

back, and removed a box of tools that he had tucked in a corner. "Don't be so sure, laddy boy. I said I'd get you to Ostia, and I mean to do just that! As for you, just stay out of what's left of my hair."

"Ben, I'm c-c-cold," said Marcus, sitting up in the wagon and rubbing his eyes.

"Well, little one, I'm sure we can do something about that. Zak, let's get a fire going."

In no time at all, Ben and Zak had gathered some dry twigs and broken tree limbs and had a fire blazing. Zak rubbed his hands together, holding them over the flames. "Ah! You can't beat a good campfire. Warm enough for you, Marcus?"

"Yes, Zak. Thank you." Marcus sat hugging his knees, looking into the fire.

"Hey, Zak, we've collected more wood," said Cyrus.

Justin and Anna and Cyrus each were carrying a huge armload of wood. They stacked the wood neatly nearby so it would be ready to feed to the fire to keep it going.

Cyrus flipped some of his sticks into the air and began juggling them. This kept everyone amused for a bit, but it was getting much colder. So the children and Helena huddled around the fire while Ben and Zak watched Milo repair the broken wheel. From a short distance, of course.

"Where did the leaders in the Ostian underground find that old smuggler, Ben?" Zak asked.

"No one knows much about Milo, except that he's

traveled just about every road, footpath, and goat trail in the Roman Empire."

"Humph!" said Zak, suitably unimpressed.

"Look, there goes another one!" shouted Cyrus, leaning back and pointing up at a shooting star in the sky.

"Wow!" Anna said.

"And another!" cried Cyrus.

Ben walked over to the fire and sat down next to Marcus.

"Ben, why do stars fall?" Marcus asked.

"Well, I can't tell you the answer to that one, Marcus. That's a question for the Magi," Ben said.

"Who's the Magi?" asked Justin.

"Yes, I'd like to know too," broke in Anna.

"Go on, Ben, tell them," said Helena. "We could be here awhile."

Zak joined them, sitting close enough to the fire to stay warm but off to one side so he could keep an eye on Milo.

"Well, the Magi are men who study the stars. In fact, a group of them play a part in one of my favorite stories. It is a very special story and quite new, too. So different from the ones I usually tell about Jesus. Come on, huddle together, and I'll tell you."

Ben looked at each one of the eager young faces, then started the story. "A long time ago, when my father was still just a boy, several Magi discovered a new star."

"In the sky?"

"Yes, Marcus, in the sky," chuckled Ben, ruffling Marcus's hair as the youngster snuggled back against Ben's large paunch. "But this star had a special meaning. These Magi knew somehow that the new star meant that a special king had been born. So they decided to follow the star in hopes of finding this new king.

"It took them a long time. The Magi traveled for nearly two years, always following the star, before they finally came to Jerusalem, the capital city of Israel.

"Unfortunately, there was already a king living in Israel at the time. His name was Herod. He was a vain man, a bit like our Nero. He was also very cruel like Nero, and moody. He lived in constant fear that someone would steal his throne. So he was very cruel to his subjects."

"Why would someone want to steal his chair, Ben?" Cyrus asked.

"Not his chair. His throne, his seat of power, his right to be the king."

"Oh."

"Hush, Cyrus," said Anna. "Let Ben continue."

"Thank you, Anna. As I was saying, Herod was afraid that someone would steal his kingdom from him. Of course, his staff all thought he was slightly mad. The idea that someone could steal his throne did seem to be a little crazy. After all, he had soldiers to protect him. But Herod was still worried. And he was willing to do anything to remain king—even kill his own wife and family if necessary.

"Well, as you can imagine, the appearance of the Magi in Jerusalem made Herod very suspicious. He had been told that they were riding toward Jerusalem. As soon as they arrived, he sent for them. 'Why have you come to Jerusalem?' he asked.

"The Magi replied, 'We have come to worship the child who was born to be the king of the Jews. Do you know where we might find him?'

"Herod was furious and stormed out of the room. He called a meeting of his advisers.

"At the meeting, the advisers sat around a large table, and Herod thumped the table angrily. 'I am the king of the Jews, their *only* king.' Herod thumped the table again. 'Where can I find this other "king" they speak of?'

"The elders all looked at each other and discussed the news that the Magi had brought about a new king. They studied scrolls and other important documents. Finally the eldest adviser stood up, turned to Herod, and said, 'He is to be found in Bethlehem. Just as the prophet Micah predicted, eight hundred years ago.'

"'Bethlehem, you say?' said Herod, with a wicked grin. 'Well done.'

"Herod immediately summoned the Magi to appear before him again at the palace.

"'I am advised that the child you seek is in Bethlehem. When you find him, come back and tell me where he is …' Herod paused and grinned. '… for I too would like to worship him.'

"Then King Herod asked the Magi one more question, a very important question: "When did you first learn about this child?'

"'We first saw the star two years ago,' they told King Herod.

"And so the Magi, riding their camels, traveled the road out of Jerusalem to the nearby village of Bethlehem. There the child, who would have been about two years old by then, lived with his parents, Mary and Joseph.

"It was Joseph who answered the door when the Magi knocked. When he let them in, they saw the child sitting on Mary's lap.

"They knelt before him and gave him presents—gold fit for a king, frankincense for worship, and last, a very unusual present, myrrh. This was a strange present because myrrh is usually used during the burial of the dead. But it was one of the presents they brought. Perhaps the Magi knew that some sorrow would befall that little boy. Who knows. They never said.

"Because later that night, one of the Magi had what can only be described as a very vivid nightmare. He awoke immediately and discussed it with his friends. And then, just as suddenly as they had arrived, they left, leaving Mary, Joseph, and their little boy behind."

"Ben?"

"Yes, Justin?"

"Where did they go?"

"Well, no one knows where the Magi went, but one thing is certain—they did not return to Jerusalem or to King Herod's palace."

"Was Herod angry?"

"Angry! He was livid! When Herod realized the Magi had tricked him, he flew into one of his terrible rages. He ranted and raved at his advisers and everyone else who would listen. He called the Magi 'sorcerers' and accused them of trying to hide the child from him.

"'So be it!' Herod said. 'By the time I am finished, they'll wish they'd delivered him to me on a plate!'

"Then Herod did a very wicked thing. He ordered the captain of the palace guard to assemble his men immediately. He told them to search all of Bethlehem and kill every male child who was two years old or younger. Not one was to escape alive."

"But that's terrible, Ben," said Anna, clearly upset.

None of the others said a word. It was not like Ben to tell a sad story, and this one had taken them all by surprise. Even Zak was silent.

For a long time they stared at the flames and listened to the popping and crackling of the fire as sparks burst into the air. Somehow, looking for shooting stars had lost its appeal.

Suddenly, the silence was broken by a great howling. "OOOUUU!" The children jumped up.

What could it be?

Chapter 5

Empty-handed

Back in Rome, the evil Emperor Nero was quietly pondering in the private chamber of his palace. He was looking up at the moon. "Perfect, it is simply perfect."

"Oh yes, Caesar," repeated Snivilus Grovilus, Nero's chief groveler: "It is perfect indeed." Snivilus, who was at the other side of the room, had absolutely no idea what Nero was talking about, but he knew he had to agree.

"Yes, a full moon is just what we need."

"Yes, Caesar, absolutely Caesar, I couldn't agree more. A full moon. What better? There is nothing better than a full moon. Er? Did you say *need*? May I ask what for, Caesar?" inquired Snivilus, cautiously.

Nero raised his eyes in disbelief: "For rounding up Christians, you stupid, groveling little toad." He blurted: "Even Christians can't sneak around in the dark when there is no darkness."

"How observant and how right Caesar is," wheedled Snivilus, now realising what Nero was referring to. "It's a perfect moon for Christian catching."

"Yes." Nero grinned. "Well done, Snivilus, *Christian-catching*. I like that."

Snivilus positively glowed in this faint praise.

"And out catching Christians are my special, crack crew of Christian-catchers. Trained by my own hand, they will not let us down."

"A … a special team?" queried Snivilus. "Is it a platoon of men?"

"No, not a platoon," replied Caesar.

"A garrison of soldiers, then?"

"Not a garrison." Nero grinned, enjoying the guessing game.

"An army of infantry, then."

"Wrong again. Keep trying."

"Then it must be the Elite Imperial Guard," added Snivilus, confidently.

"Pooh! Elite Imperial Guard indeed. Those ninnies couldn't catch a cold."

"Tch! No. What am I saying? Of course not. What a silly suggestion that was." Snivilus winced.

"Silly indeed. But you still can't guess," said Nero.

"Well, that is because your eminence, in his ever intelligent wisdom, has chosen to keep his crack team a secret. And so he should too. Caesars need to have secrets. It is secrets that make them great. *'Caesar's Christian Catchers'* should be the best-kept secret in the whole of Rome."

Nero was a little miffed that Snivilus wasn't going to guess anymore. "Well," he said, "I am great. And I suppose I should have some secrets. But what is the point of having great ideas if you can't tell anyone how great you are for thinking them up?"

Snivilus was just about to turn his mind to this puzzle when Stouticus, the fattest soldier in the whole of the Roman army, entered the room. As he walked, his whole body wobbled. "Hail, Caesar!" he bellowed.

"What do you want?" Caesar barked back. "If it is more rations, the answer is no."

"Oh!" said Stouticus, letting the thought of food distract him from his message for just a second. "Hail, Caesar," he repeated.

"You already said that. What do you want? You know, Stouticus, you are such a buffoon I have a mind to feed you to the lions, and a hefty feast you would be too."

Stouticus gulped and smiled weakly. "The three horsemen have returned."

As Stouticus spoke, the horsemen who had chased Milo's wagon on the road to Ostia were tying up their horses in the Imperial stable.

"Then why didn't you say so, you dolt. It's lucky for you. My horsemen will no doubt have many Christians for the lions to eat. It would be a shame to spoil their appetite."

A smile returned to Stouticus's face. "I ... I'll just send them in, shall I?" He gulped.

"Of course, you fat fool."

As the three horsemen entered the room, Nero turned to Snivilus and said, "Shut your eyes. As you have already suggested, these men need to be kept secret."

Snivilus was upset, but did as he was told.

Then Nero turned to the three horsemen: "Gentlemen. How nice it is to be dealing with men as able as you. I always say you equestrian types are a breed apart, such wise men. Do I not, Snivilus?"

Snivilus still had his eyes closed and he longed to take a peep, but didn't dare. "Oh yes, Caesar. Always, Caesar. Why, only the other day you said . . ."

"Oh shut up, Snivilus," retorted Nero, before turning again to the horsemen. "So tell me, gentlemen. How many Christians did you bag? Twenty?"

The horsemen hesitated. "Ah …"

"Thirty, then?" said Nero eagerly.

"Uh . . ."

"Forty? Is it forty? Oh, tell me, tell me. I can't bear the suspense."

The horsemen glanced at each other, anxiously. "Well, er … none."

"None! NONE!" exploded Nero. "What do you mean none? FOOLS! I am surrounded by fools and nincompoops. How can you come back here and say none? Crack Christian-catchers indeed."

One of the horsemen stepped forward bravely. "We were outmaneuvered. They are employing some very smart people to help them escape. But don't worry, sir, we chased them into the wilderness. They are still out there, and the wolves will get them."

"Wolves? Well, I suppose it's better than nothing. But what about my hungry lions? Stouticus! Stouticus? Now where's he gone?"

Stouticus had seen the sense of leaving, long before the horsemen had the chance to tell their news. "Phew!" he said out loud. "That was a close one. I love to eat dinner, but don't want to be it. Perhaps Nihilus or Tacticus would have some work for me. Out of town, perhaps. Then again, maybe I will just go down to the kitchen and see if there are any little scraps. Lunch was ages ago, and it is a long wait until dinnertime ..." Stouticus kept talking to himself as he waddled as far away from Nero as possible.

Chapter 6

A Howl
in the Night

"W-w-what was that?" asked Cyrus, anxiously.

"OOOUUU! OOOUUU!" went the caterwaul again.

"Wolf!" said Milo, looking up from his work on the wheel. "We're in wolf country."

"W-wolf? You mean there are wolves here?" asked Cyrus.

"Yes, of course," said Milo. "Don't you know the story of Romulus and Remus?"

"N-no," said Cyrus.

"Remind me to tell you sometime."

"But, Milo, what do we do? He sounds very close," Cyrus said, looking anxiously up at the trees on the hill behind them.

"Probably is. Probably came down for a look."

Cyrus was beginning to panic, and Justin and Anna didn't look too happy either. Little Marcus had fallen asleep again.

"Will it attack us?" asked Anna nervously.

"No, don't worry," Milo said, turning back to his work. "It's just some nosy old wolf howling at the moon. The fire will keep it away."

"I sure hope so," said Cyrus.

"Me too," said Justin.

They all sat staring at the fire, turning every once in a while to nervously look off in the direction from where the howling had come. After a while, when there was only silence, Anna said, "Joseph and Mary must have escaped, but how?"

"Yes, Ben. Tell us the rest," Justin said.

"Well," continued Ben, "the same night that King Herod ordered his men to kill all the young boys, Joseph was warned by an angel of the Lord."

"How?"

"In another terrible dream."

"What, like the dream the Magi had?"

"Yes, Cyrus, it was probably very much like the dream the Magi had."

"What happened in the dream?"

"Joseph dreamed that Herod was standing before his soldiers, shouting, 'I am the king of the Jews! Their only king!' Then Joseph saw mean-looking guards marching, with swords drawn, going from house to house.

"Joseph woke up in a sweat. He knew the dream was an urgent message, a message for him to get Mary and the baby away from Bethlehem. They had to escape. They had to leave that very night.

"Soon after Joseph's dream, Herod's soldiers broke into homes all over Bethlehem, killing all the boys aged two and under. It was terrible. Mothers and fathers tried to shield their children. Some even tried to fight the Romans off, but to no avail. One by one the children were murdered.

"Then, all over Bethlehem, you could hear the sound of mothers weeping for their dead children."

"But what about Mary and Joseph?" Anna asked. "What about their little boy?"

"Soldiers, with swords drawn, barged into the house that Joseph and Mary lived in too," Ben said. "They didn't knock or anything. They just kicked the door in. When they got inside, the house was empty."

"They did escape," said Justin, relieved.

"Yes. Joseph, Mary, and their little boy had managed to escape just in time."

Justin, Cyrus, and Anna could scarcely look at each other. Their eyes were bright with tears.

"Is there no happy ending, Ben?" asked Cyrus.

"Well, yes there is, Cyrus. Mary, Joseph, and the baby escaped to Egypt, and from then on, great things began to happen."

Justin felt sure he didn't need to ask, but he did anyway, just to check. "Ben, w-was Joseph's and Mary's baby … the baby Jesus?"

"Why, yes, Justin. It was the baby Jesus. Didn't I say that?"

"No!" everyone chorused.

"Well, I meant to say that. How could I have left that out?" Ben said as he slapped his forehead and chuckled. "But that means I haven't told you the whole story."

Helena smiled at her husband. "Yes, Ben, you missed the beginning."

"Tell us, tell us," the children cried in unison.

"I will, but first we must see how Milo is doing. Don't forget, we are on our way to Ostia."

Zak was still very suspicious of Milo and he checked the wagon thoroughly, but he couldn't see anything wrong with it.

"All set then?" asked Milo, grinning. "All checks done?"

"Huh!" grunted Zak. "I'll be watching you."

"That's good," replied Milo. "Then you might learn to behave like an adult."

Zak was annoyed that Milo should treat him like a child, but resolved to keep an eye on the old wagon driver.

"All right, everybody. Time to get rolling." As he waited on the others, Milo chuckled as he patted his horse. "What's that, Regis? No, that's not it. The Rabbi says to the innkeeper: 'Do you serve duck?' It was the innkeeper who said … Oh, never mind, old boy, it was a dumb joke anyway."

Zak shook his head. "How can we trust a man who tells his horse dumb jokes?"

"Hold on, everybody!"

Milo the wagon driver was used to danger

Helena tells about Mary and Joseph

Ordinary shepherds were the first to see Jesus

Zak doesn't trust Milo

Milo finds a way

But why does he go off to the inn?

A star like one when Jesus was born

Magi looking for a king

And another king who was ready to kill

They find him, but not at Herod's palace

Jesus' family were in danger too

That very night an angel warned Joseph in a dream

They escaped to Egypt

"I knew it was a trap!"

"Goodbye" to Milo

Just then, as Milo climbed on to the wagon, Regis suddenly shook his tousled mane and whinnied uncontrollably; the whole wagon began to shake.

"Ah!" said Milo, with a chuckle, "so you get it now. It must be the way I tell them."

The gang finally got on their way.

Chapter 7

Meanwhile, Back in Rome

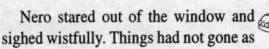

Nero stared out of the window and sighed wistfully. Things had not gone as he had expected. "I am so utterly, utterly bored, Snivilus. Why am I so bored?"

"Uh! Well! Um!"

"Exactly! I am bored because nothing is happening. I send my crack Christian-catchers out and they come back empty-handed. I wanted to have a little action, a little sport. Instead those dimwits leave the Christians to the wolves." Nero looked up at the full moon. "Why, I bet those wolves are howling at the moon right now, before they move in on the Christians. Oh, how I want to see that sport."

"Gulp!" went Snivilus. He hated wolves, and was hoping if Caesar went he would go alone.

"But I want even more to feed the Christians to my lions," pouted Nero. "Are there no Christians in Rome anymore?"

"Well, I don't really know," Snivilus replied. "Perhaps

34

they have all gone off to the coast."

"Pah!" said Nero in disgust as he slammed the window shut. "Christians don't go to the coast. They go off to spread more lies about me and to tell stories about that carpenter of theirs to other Christians. If we don't stop them, there will be more Christians than Nero-lovers." Suddenly Nero stopped ranting. "But wait. Perhaps you have something, after all."

"I do? I mean I do, your Eminence," said Snivilus. "But what?"

"Oh, don't be an imbecile all your life, Snivilus. Do I have to spell it out?"

"Well," said Snivilus, "that's why you are Caesar, oh wise one. You're the one with all the wisdom."

"True, true," said Nero, as he preened himself in front of a large mirror. "I suppose I am a true genius."

"The truest!" added Snivilus.

"Yes, true, you can see it in my eyes. Every time I look in the mirror I see my own genius. Ah, well," sighed Nero. "But back to business," he snapped. "Christian-catching business. Call Tacticus."

Tacticus entered Nero's chamber at Snivilus's request.

"Hail, Caesar!"

"Tacticus, I want you to go and look for Christians in the countryside on the way to the coast. They may be there, and if they are, they will be spreading their malicious little stories. They think I can't reach them there, but I'll show them. We'll hunt them down."

Tacticus hesitated. He had become fond of the Christians. Two Christian children, Anna and Justin, had saved his life when a fellow Roman guard had left him to die.

Nero ignored Tacticus's hesitation. "We'll begin in Ostia. Organize some soldiers to begin the search."

"Yes, Caesar," agreed Tacticus, and he turned to leave the chamber.

Snivilus sidled over to congratulate Nero. "Brilliant. Truly brilliant, Caesar," he said. "How could those Christians think they would ever escape the great Caesar? Why, Caesar has the brain power of … of …"

"Yes, Snivilus?"

"Of . . . a thousand men?" hesitated Snivilus.

"Only a thousand?" asked Nero calmly, before turning to Tacticus again. "Snivilus will be coming with you. Can you point the wolves out to him?"

Snivilus gulped, a look of terror on his face.

"Oh, and do take that oaf Stouticus with you," added Nero. "He eats too much in Rome. Every time I want some of my favorite pastries, I find that fat clod has already eaten the lot."

"Yes, Caesar," replied Tacticus.

Chapter 8

Let's Go, Milo

Zakkai walked over to where Milo was working on the wheel, but before he could say anything, he overheard the old man talking to someone.

"No, you've got it all wrong, Regis …"

"Uh, Milo," Zak said, hesitantly.

Seeming not to have heard, Milo continued, "… we've gone over all this before."

Zakkai looked a little startled, then disgusted.

Milo was alone. He was just talking to his horse again.

Shaking his head, Zak muttered to himself, "What are we doing here? This old dolt is goofy, and he probably couldn't hear a thunderbolt if it hit him in the ear."

"Watch it, sonny," Milo said quietly. He looked over his shoulder at a surprised Zak. "It's a long walk to Ostia. Want to try it?"

"Uh, sorry, old-timer. I … I mean we … were just wondering if …"

"And I said I wanted you to stay out of my hair. I'll call you when I've finished."

As Zak turned, he heard Milo say, "So anyway, Regis, the reason they had to join the others …"

"Great," Zak said as he walked back to the campfire.

"What did Milo say, Zak?" asked Ben.

"You don't want to know. He's still talking to that old horse as if the horse understands him. But it does look like he's putting the finishing touches on the wheel. We should soon be on our way."

"Ah, that's good. Did you hear that, everyone? We'll be on our way soon."

"Thank goodness," said Cyrus as the wolf, sounding just a bit closer this time, again let out a chilling howl.

In a few minutes, Milo joined the gang around the campfire. "Okay. Time we were moving. The wheel's fixed for now. If I need to, I can do a better job when we get to Ostia." Then he walked back to the wagon and climbed up onto the driver's seat.

"I'm ready," said Cyrus, as he quickly jumped up into the wagon.

"You know, Regis," said Milo, smiling, "I don't think our young juggler friend is all that keen on the thought of wolves."

Regis whinnied and Milo chuckled. "All aboard!" he called.

Soon the wagon was bouncing along the rocky, dry riverbed.

"Whoever heard of driving down a riverbed," grumbled Zak, who had been taking a drink of water when the wagon bumped over a big rock, spilling water down the front of his tunic. "Was this your idea, Milo, or did Regis suggest it?"

"Very funny. Regis is just a horse," Milo said.

Regis whinnied and tossed his head.

"No, Regis," Milo said, leaning forward toward the horse, "I didn't say there was anything wrong with being a horse. I was just saying …"

"One thing's for sure," said Ben, "Nero's soldiers will never spot us down here."

Milo glanced in Zak's direction. "Exactly. Laddy boy, I know these parts better than an old dog knows its fleas. You can take it from me, there is absolutely no quicker way to Caesarea Philippi than straight down this riverbed."

The others exchanged questioning looks. Caesarea Philippi?

"But we're going to Ostia," Justin said, with a bit of concern showing in his voice.

Milo sat up straighter and kept looking ahead. "I know that," he said. Then, in a hushed voice, he said to Regis, "Psst, Ostia."

Regis whinnied and veered to the right, taking one of the dried-up tributaries.

In the back of the wagon, Helena and the kids leaned back and looked up at the stars. The sky seemed filled with stars. They seemed brighter than ever, and every once in a while, a shooting star streaked a silvery path.

"Marcus, can you see the shooting stars?" Helena asked. "Are you awake?"

It was so dark, she couldn't see him.

There was no reply.

"Ben, is Marcus still asleep?"

"I don't know. Isn't he with you?"

"No," Helena said, her voice rising with worry. "I thought he was with you. Justin," she cried, "where's your brother?"

Chapter 9

Marcus Is Missing!

"I don't know!" Justin cried. "Maybe we left him behind! He was curled up, sleeping."

"Stop, Milo!" shouted Helena. "Stop!"

Regis reacted immediately and stopped without waiting for Milo to say "Whoa."

Justin jumped down from the back of the wagon, but Zak grabbed his arm. "You can't go running back alone, Justin. It's too dangerous."

"Let me go! He's my brother!" he shouted, shaking off Zak's hand.

"Zak's right, Justin," Ben said. "There may still be wolves back there. We'll go together."

"Wolves! Hurry!" Justin cried, starting to run back the way they had come.

"Helena, you stay here with Anna, Cyrus, and Milo," Ben said. "It will be quicker if we go on foot. It's not that far."

"Oh, Ben, be careful."

"We will," said Ben, before turning to Zak. "Okay. Let's go."

No one in the wagon said a word as they watched as Ben and Zak caught up to Justin. Then the trio hurried back along the dried-up riverbed. Soon they disappeared around a bend.

"M-Milo," said an anxious Cyrus, "what if the wolves get Marcus, I mean what if ..."

"Oh, Cyrus, you shouldn't think such bad thoughts," said the old man.

"But wolves are dangerous, aren't they?"

"Yes, they can be, but it's only when they're hunting for food or if their young pups are threatened. Let me tell you about Romulus and Remus."

"You mentioned them before. Who are they?"

Milo didn't know if the legend of Romulus and Remus was a true story, but that didn't matter right then. He could see he had to do something to keep their minds off little Marcus.

"Well," began Milo, "legend has it that before Rome was built, there was a woman called Rhea Silvia whose father was a king. Unfortunately, her father had been wrongfully ousted from his throne by his wicked brother.

"Anyway, Rhea Silvia had twin boys. She called them Romulus and Remus. How she loved those boys. She would wrap them up in swaddling clothes and give them milk and sing to them.

"But she also had this wicked uncle, the same uncle

who had treated her father so badly. His name was Amulius. He knew that one day, when the boys were old enough, they would come to claim their birthright, which he had stolen.

"So, do you know what he did?"

"No," said Cyrus.

"Well, the wicked uncle Amulius threw Rhea Silvia in prison and then hurled the twins into the river Tiber."

"Oh, that's terrible," said Helena. "That poor woman and her children."

"Yes, quite," said Milo.

"Did the twins drown?" asked Anna.

"No. That's the whole point. Listen and I'll tell you. Romulus and Remus sailed down the Tiber for a bit. Then they were washed ashore and were looked after by a she-wolf until a royal herdsman rescued them."

"A wolf?"

"That's what I said."

"And she didn't eat them?"

"Nope. She fed them with her own milk."

"Then the herdsman took them back to their mother?"

"No, I'm afraid not. She was in prison, remember. So the herdsman and his wife looked after the boys for many years. And when they grew up, Romulus built a city on Palatine Hill and called it ..." he stopped in the middle of the sentence.

"Rome!" cried Anna excitedly. "He must have called it Rome."

"How right you are, youngster," Milo said with a smile. "So you see, if there were no wolves, there would be no Rome. That she-wolf did Romulus and Remus a big favor."

"Well, let's hope Marcus doesn't have to see a wolf, far less get looked after by one," said Helena anxiously. "I wonder where Ben and the boys are now."

* * *

It was lucky that Regis was usually a pretty slow horse, because Ben and Zak and Justin didn't have far to go along the dried-up riverbed.

"We'll soon be there," Ben said. "We camped up there, in that clearing just ahead," he said, pointing.

"Oh, I hope Marcus is all right," said Justin. "I will never forgive myself if—"

"Justin," said Ben calmly. "He's all right. It wasn't your fault."

"But I promised my father I would look after him. I promised my father we would stay together … until …" Tears welled up in his eyes.

"Justin, I'm sure he will be just where we left him," Ben said reassuringly.

"The fire will be out! He'll be cold!" Justin cried.

"And if there's no fire, there is a greater chance that the wolves will come," Zak said, not thinking how his words would frighten Justin.

"Hey, you two. Have some faith," Ben said.

The three left the riverbed and walked up the steep riverbank, heading toward the clearing.

"Look, over there, there's still a little bit of fire," said Zak.

"Shh!" Ben said, holding his arms out to prevent Justin and Zak from walking any closer.

"W-what … what is … that?" Justin whispered. "By the fire, look …"

Chapter 10

The Protector

"It's a wolf," said Ben quietly, still holding his arms out to keep Zak and Justin from rushing forward.

"I ... I don't see Marcus," Justin said, his voice rising in panic.

"No, he's there," Ben said. "See? He's curled up against the wolf."

"What shall we do? We can't disturb it," said Zak.

"Ben, I'm scared," whispered Justin.

"Hush, I'm thinking."

After watching the wolf carefully for a few minutes, Ben, Zak, and Justin started inching forward, treading warily toward the sleeping Marcus and the wolf. They got to within a few yards when the wolf uttered a very low, threatening growl.

"It's seen us," whispered Ben. "Don't move."

The three of them froze in their tracks.

"What do we do now, Ben?" hissed Zak.

Ben had no idea. He was afraid that if they went any closer, the wolf might attack them. Or hurt Marcus. He didn't have a stick or anything to defend them or to scare off the wolf.

Just then, Marcus awoke and stretched. He leaned his head against the wolf and began stroking its back and neck and scratching an ear. The wolf nuzzled under Marcus's chin and the youngster giggled, "Hey, that tickles. Cut it out."

It seemed like an age before Marcus looked up, but when he did he shouted, "Justin! Ben! Zak! I knew you'd come back for me!"

Marcus got up and ran to his brother, who hugged him long and hard. "Oh, Marcus, you're safe. I'm so sorry, I'm so sorry," Justin said, still holding his brother tightly.

They all started walking backwards, away from the wolf, still keeping a wary eye on the animal.

"Can my dog come?" Marcus said, looking back at the wolf.

The wolf was standing now, facing them, its head down a little. Its eyes gleamed wildly in the moonlight.

"A dog, huh!" said Zak with less than his usual confidence. "That dog is staring at us and thinking about breakfast. Shall we run?"

"No," Ben said quickly. "Just back away slowly."

The wolf was no longer growling. It watched Marcus and Justin for a while, then, tilting its head back, let out an enormous "OOOUUU!" For a few more moments it watched the group, then turned and headed back toward the woods.

"Well," said Ben, "I have never seen anything like that in my life."

"Bye," shouted Marcus. "And thanks!"

The wolf stopped, howled again, and then it was gone.

"I wish I could have kept that dog," Marcus said, grinning. "It kept me warm."

"Oh, you're safe now," said Justin, again hugging his little brother. "Were you scared?"

"A little. I remember being cold, but I heard you talking and I went back to sleep. Then, when I woke up again and looked around, there was no one here. I started to cry … a little … but I stayed where I was because I knew you'd come back for me. I knew it. I just sat there, looking around. It was really cold. And pretty soon the dog came along and kept me warm. I guess I fell asleep again."

Ben didn't know if Helena and the others had heard the wolf cries back at the wagon. He hoped they had not.

"Come on, let's head back," he said, taking Marcus from his brother and lifting the little boy onto his shoulders.

Chapter 11

The Wonderful Story, Interrupted

At the wagon, Cyrus was still quizzing Milo. "Did the twins ever see the she-wolf again?"

"I don't know, Cyrus. I—" Milo thought he heard something, a crunching sound. He turned his head so he could hear better.

"Here they come! Here they come!" shouted Anna. "And Marcus is with them!"

"Oh, he's safe, he's safe," said Helena quietly, looking down and closing her eyes briefly. A tear rolled down her cheek, and she dabbed it quickly before anyone would notice.

Cyrus turned to Milo. "I wonder if Marcus saw a wolf."

"Oh, I expect not," chuckled a relieved Milo.

With Marcus tucked safely in the wagon between Ben and Helena, the gang finally got underway—again.

"Ostia, here we come!" shouted Ben.

"At long last," added Zak. He wouldn't admit to

anyone how much leaving Marcus behind had frightened him.

Helena hugged Marcus, then continued to hold him close to her. He didn't resist.

"Helena?"

"Yes, Marcus?"

"When I was half asleep in front of the campfire, I thought I heard Ben telling a story about Bethlehem."

"That's right," said Helena as she ran her fingers through Marcus's hair. "It was about Mary and Joseph and the baby Jesus in Bethlehem."

"Were you ever in Bethlehem?"

"No, but my parents once passed through Nazareth. That's the town in Judea where Mary and Joseph lived."

"But I thought Jesus was born in Bethlehem," piped in Anna, who was quick to pick up the name of the different town.

"Yes. Why was he born in Bethlehem if they lived in Nazareth?" Justin asked.

"Tell us the rest of the story," Cyrus insisted.

"Yes, yes," said Marcus, who wasn't a bit sleepy after his long nap back by the campfire.

"Well …"

"Go on, Helena," said a smiling Ben. "Tell the children. Now that Marcus is back, safe and sound, it is a good time to hear the wonderful story."

"Well, if you're sure you want to hear it." Helena hesitated.

"Yes!" everyone cried in unison.

"All right then." Helena smiled. "Yes, Anna, you are right, Jesus was born in Bethlehem, but the story really begins before that.

"You see, in those days Joseph worked in Nazareth as a carpenter. He had become engaged to be married to Mary, who lived nearby, in the same town.

"Nazareth is only a small town. And, for that matter, Israel is only a small country. But, as Ben will confirm, the people hated being ruled by the Roman emperor. Just like today, they longed to be free and dreamed of the day when God would send them a great leader. Some people were prepared to fight, but others, like Mary, prayed.

"One night, when Mary was saying her prayers, she heard a voice that said, 'Peace be with you, Mary. The Lord is with you and has blessed you.'

"Mary was confused by what the voice said and wondered what it meant. Then she heard the voice again.

"'God is pleased with you. You will have a son and will call him Jesus. God will make him a king, and his kingdom will never end.'

"Well, Mary was now very confused. She could not think how this could be, since she had no husband.

"'There is nothing God cannot do,' came the reply to her questions. 'His spirit will come to you and his powers will rest on you. The child will be a holy child. He will be the Son of God.'

"Mary bowed and replied, 'I am the Lord's servant.

Let it happen to me as you have said.'

"And so it did. Mary soon learned that she was going to have a baby. Of course, Mary was still not married, and when Joseph found out that she was going to have a baby, Joseph thought the right thing to do was to quietly break off the engagement."

Without warning, the wagon stopped and Milo climbed down from his seat.

Zak, who had been sitting in the back with the rest of them, jumped out and ran after the old man. "Hey, Milo! Why have we stopped?"

That's when he noticed that Milo had parked the wagon outside a seedy-looking tavern.

"You folks stay here," said Milo. "I'll be right back."

Zak grabbed his arm. "Wait! Where are you going?"

"Where does it look like I'm going? I have to talk to someone inside to get the location of this secret meeting of yours."

Milo pulled his arm free and walked toward the tavern, opened the door, and disappeared inside.

Zak was left standing in the middle of the street. But he had had a good look inside the tavern. And he didn't like what he saw.

He walked back to the wagon and climbed in. "Ben, I don't like this. Some of those people in that tavern look pretty shady to me. You should have seen how they were eyeing us."

Ben hesitated, then said, "Milo's brought us this far."

He paused and put a hand on Zak's shoulder. "I'm sure he knows what he's doing."

"That's what I'm afraid of. Look!"

Four Roman soldiers had just come out of the tavern and were looking around.

"Soldiers!" Ben said.

"Yes, soldiers."

"It's maybe nothing," Ben said.

"And maybe something!" Zak insisted.

Ben and Zak looked at each other apprehensively.

Chapter 12

And the Rest of the Story

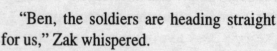

"Ben, the soldiers are heading straight for us," Zak whispered.

As the soldiers approached the wagon, Zak reached down by his side. Ben grabbed his arm. "Leave the sword, Zak. We have to think about the children."

As the soldiers came closer, Zak heard one say, "All day long Nero has us out looking for Christians. Thank goodness we stumbled on this tavern. The food was pretty good. And I was so hungry."

"Stouticus," said another soldier, "you are always hungry."

"Not always. Not when I'm in Rome. In Rome I visit Ben the baker."

"Stouticus!" muttered Ben under his breath as he slid back into the shadows of the covered wagon. "He might recognize me."

"That Ben," they heard Stouticus say, "he bakes the best pastries in the whole of Rome. They melt in your mouth. People come from miles around to buy them.

His shop is always full of people. Ooh, I could eat some right now. Even though I just ate. Especially the almond ones … or the apple … no, the vanilla. What a baker. As soon as I get to Rome, I'm going to stop at the bakery. Even Nero loves Ben's pastries."

Ben, who had looked a little bit uncomfortable at Stouticus's compliments, gulped at the sound of Nero's name. Then he watched as Stouticus and the other soldiers walked right in front of the wagon and headed for their horses, which had been tied nearby.

"Oh well, best get back to work, I suppose," Stouticus said. "Someone in the tavern said he saw a campfire up by the dried-up stream. We'd better take a look."

The soldiers mounted their horses and rode off.

"Hey," Stouticus could be heard saying, just before they rounded a bend in the road, "you don't think there are wolves up there, do you?"

The gang in the wagon couldn't hear the reply.

"Phew!" said Zak as everyone relaxed.

"That was a close one," said Cyrus.

"Too close!" Zak said. "Come on, Ben, let's get out of here. We can find the meeting on our own. That old coot Milo is just asking for trouble, parking the wagon here."

"Milo said he would be right back," Justin said. "I think we should trust him."

"Me too," added Anna.

"Me too," piped in little Marcus.

Ben pondered their problem, then said, "We'll wait

just awhile longer."

Zak was clearly annoyed. "But Ben ..."

"Helena, continue with your story," Ben said.

Zak shook his head, then sat down in the wagon, resigned to the wait.

Helena gathered the children around her and launched into the story again.

"As you will remember," she said, calmly, "Joseph had ended the engagement because Mary was going to have a baby. Well, one night, not long after he'd called off the wedding, Joseph had a dream, and in that dream a voice said:

"'Joseph, you mustn't be afraid to marry Mary. God is the father of her baby, and you shall call him Jesus, for he will save his people from their sins.'

"So the very next morning, Joseph went to see Mary and told her that they should go ahead with the wedding after all, just as they had planned. So they did.

"However, before the baby was due to be born, Caesar Augustus, the Roman emperor at that time, devised a plan to make it easier for his tax collectors to gather in the taxes. He sent out an order to every part of his empire, saying the people had to have their names put on a register.

"This really upset many Jews. It reminded them that they were not free. Their country was occupied by Romans and they were being forced to support the Roman Empire.

"To make sure there were no riots, Caesar Augustus also decreed that to register, everyone had to return to the place where they had been born.

"This meant that Mary and Joseph had to go south, to Bethlehem, in the province of Judea. Bethlehem also is known as the City of David because it is the place where the great shepherd king David was born.

"The journey to Bethlehem was a long and difficult one, especially for Mary, who was still pregnant. By the time she and Joseph arrived in Bethlehem, the baby was almost ready to be born. The town was very crowded. They was no room in the place for them to stay. They had to go down to the stable, where animals were kept. And that's where the baby Jesus was born—in that stable.

"After he was born, Mary and Joseph wrapped the baby in warm clothes. How they must have adored their little boy.

"That same night, not far out of town, some shepherds were tending their flocks when suddenly they were bathed in a bright light and an angel appeared. They were very frightened, but the angel said:

"'Don't be afraid. I have good news for you. Today your Savior has been born, who is Christ, the Lord. You will find him in the town, lying in a manger.'

"The sky was ablaze with light and the shepherds could hear singing. 'Glory to God in heaven, and peace to all people on earth,' the voices sang.

"The shepherds were convinced that the Lord had,

indeed, sent this message to them. So they set off for Bethlehem.

"When the shepherds got to the stable, they told Mary and Joseph what they had heard about Jesus. Mary listened quietly and kept the things she heard in her heart, and she continued to think about them.

"Eight days later, Mary and Joseph named their child Jesus, just as God's messenger had told them to do."

"That was a great story, Helena," Anna said. "Thank you for telling us about Bethlehem."

"You're welcome, Anna. Do you know what is one of my favorite things about that story?"

"No, what?"

"Well, ordinary shepherds were the first to see Jesus."

"I think that whole story is my favorite story," said little Marcus.

"Mine too," boomed a stranger's voice.

Chapter 13

Traitor Milo?

At the sound of the stranger's voice, they all looked up and were startled to see a huge Roman soldier looking into the wagon, straight at Helena. Standing to one side, in the shadows, was Milo.

"I knew it was a trap! I knew it! Milo, you tricked us! Go for your sword!" Zak jumped down from the wagon, drew his sword, and faced Milo.

"Now hold on, lad. Hold on," said Milo. "This soldier is a friend, and he's going to escort you to the meeting place. It's just a short walk from here."

"Huh!" said Zak, waving his sword. "He'll escort us right to the lions. That's where he'll escort us."

The soldier broke into a huge, good-natured laugh and stepped into the light. "You must be Zakkai. He's just as you described him to me, Ben. A little taller, perhaps."

"Cassius? Cassius Marcellus! I thought I recognised that laugh!" said Ben, getting down from the wagon and reaching out with both arms to the newcomer.

"Hey, look at you, Ben, that belly gets bigger every day. You eat too many of your own scrumptious pastries."

Ben and Cassius embraced warmly, slapping each other on the back.

"You can relax, Zak. Cassius and I are old friends," Ben said, turning to his apprentice. Then he leaned into the wagon and said, "Come on out, everybody, and meet Cassius."

"You have friends who are Roman soldiers?" said little Marcus in surprise as he climbed out of the wagon. "I ... I thought Tacti—"

"Shh!" said Ben putting a finger on Marcus's lips. Then, lowering his voice, he said, "Don't look so surprised everyone. Tacticus isn't the only Christian in the Roman Guard." Ben winked, and everyone smiled.

Tacticus was a friend of theirs in Rome who had to be extra careful because not only was he a Christian, he was also a Roman centurion and one of Nero's Imperial Guards.

"Come," Cassius said. "Our meeting place is filled with friends, and they're anxious to hear your stories."

"Milo," said Ben, turning to the old man, "I don't know what we would have done without you. Thank you."

Anna put her arm through Ben's and said, "Yes, thank you, Milo."

"Oh, now, it was nothing ..."

"Oh, yes it was," said Helena, and she walked over and kissed Milo on the cheek.

"Oh, my," he said, flustered. "Come on, Regis, let's get rolling." Milo climbed up to his seat and jiggled the reins. The wagon began to move forward.

"Bye, Milo!" the children called as Milo turned the wagon around to return the way they had come.

"Bye, Milo, and thanks … A safe journey to you," Ben called as the wagon moved away.

Milo waved but kept going.

Ben and Helena and the children began walking down the street with Cassius.

Zak stood there a moment, as if undecided. Then he ran to catch up with the wagon, shouting, "Milo! Wait!"

"What is it, laddy boy?" Milo said, stopping the wagon. "Forget something?"

"Well, yes. I forgot … to thank you … and I owe you an apology."

"Ahh! … you were just looking out for your friends," Milo said, his voice no longer showing any irritation with Zak.

"Yes, but … I went a little too far." Zak's head hung in shame.

"No worries, lad. A trip like this makes everyone a little jittery," Milo reassured him. "Why once, a long time ago, when I was only a little older than you are now, a family hired me to take them across the desert road to Egypt. Real nice folks, but they'd gotten themselves into some kind of trouble and they were scared silly that I was going to turn them in."

"Come on, Zak!" called Cyrus. "We have to be on our way."

Zak was just about to turn back to the others when Milo said, "I wish I could remember their names … Jared and Myra? No, that's not it …"

"Zak!" shouted Anna. "Come on!"

"Milo, I have to go. Thanks again for everything."

"Come on, Zak!" Ben called.

"You go ahead, son," Milo said, jiggling the reins again. As Regis started slowly down the road, Milo seemed lost in his thoughts. "Jason and Miriam, no … Oh, I know. That's it. Hey, lad!" shouted Milo, turning to look back at Zak. "I remember!"

Zak kept walking, pretending he hadn't heard the old man.

"Yeah! That's right, Regis. I remember now," Milo said conversationally above the clip-clop of the horse's hooves.

Zak didn't turn around. He just shook his head and muttered, "He's still talking to that old horse."

"Joseph and Mary," Milo said a little louder, with more certainty. "That's right. That's what their names were. And they had that little boy with them."

Zak stopped dead in his tracks.

"I wonder whatever happened to those folks?" Milo said, without looking back.

Zak stood frozen in the middle of the road. "Did he say … he did … he said …"

He turned around in time to see Milo and Regis disappearing into the darkness. "Why that old buzzard, I bet he knew—"

"Wow!" said Cyrus, suddenly. "Did you see that? That was the biggest shooting star I have ever seen!"

Everyone turned to look at the sky, remembering the star that had led the Magi, many years ago, to the home of Jesus.